This book is about YOUR day.
When you see the words...

I remember...

next to a rocking chair like this,
it means that it's time for YOU
to talk about what YOU did today...
from breakfast to bedtime...
and all the stops along the way.

This book is about
finding and celebrating
the moments in a child's life.
Every day.

It is dedicated to Caroline & Elizabeth,
who have led me
to some of the greatest moments
of my own life. — RK
And to Cody and Lacey,
who continue to lead me
to mine. — WH

TRISTAN Publishing
2300 Louisiana Avenue North, Suite B
Golden Valley, Minnesota 55427

TELL ME WHAT WE DID TODAY

by Rick Kupchella

illustrated by Warren Hanson

TRISTAN Publishing

Minneapolis

This is our special time.
It's the end of the day.

We've cleaned up the room.
Put the toys all away.

And we rock in our chair...
No more games left to play.

This is the place
Where we always say...

"Tell me what we did today."

There was breakfast this morning...
Remember that part?
You came down the stairs
And you asked to do art.

But your mother said,
"Wait...

There is breakfast to eat."

And you asked for oatmeal...

And ate it —

with your FEET?!

Do you remember that part?

You had toast this morning.
And you had
Scrambled eggs.
And you had pancakes.
And bacon.

And you put it all...
on your LEGS!

Do you remember that part?

NOOOO

Tell me...
Do you remember?
What was it you had?

After breakfast this morning
We went for a walk.

First to the library.

Then to the park.

And you saw that man in the boat.
Do you remember that part?

He was sailing away. All alone on that boat.

And you swam out to meet him...
And gave him your coat!

And he said,
"This does not really
fit me at all!"
And you said
you were sorry,
'Cause he was so tall!!

Do you remember that part?

NOOOOOOOOO

Oh yeah...
We were at the library.
We were READING about

a man on a boat.

And his coat.

And it started to rain.
And we had to run home.
And we ran
through the puddles...

OOOOOOOOO

And Mom called on the phone.

And she said
she'd come home
And she'd meet us
for lunch.

And we had alligators...

on crackers!

They are so fun to munch!

Do you remember that part?

Then, after lunch...

We ran up to the store.

And we bought you some milk.

And you asked for some more.

So we got some more milk.

And then more!   And some MORE!

Until we bought all the milk that they had in the store!

And that lady kept saying,
"We don't have any more!"

So we stacked all the milk
that we had
on the floor.

Then we tried hard
to push it
right out of
the door.

But it was
too big.
And you were
too small.

And so
we came home
with no milk
at all.

Do you remember that part?

NOOO

Oh yeah...
I remember...

We did get some milk.
We drank it with lunch.

Then we took a nap...

With a kangaroo
named "Punch"!

Do you remember
that part?

He was strong
and bouncy.
And he wore a big hat.

And you laid down next to him,
And he gave you a pat.

Do you remember that part?

Tell me, do you remember...

Our nap late today?

Was it cozy?

Was it comfy?

Did you dream of places far away?

I remember... we...

Then after our nap
We sat on the dock.
At first we said nothing.

Then you started to talk.

You said,
"Look at that bird.
I love how they fly.
I really wish I could fly
Just as high."

Then that bird
turned around.

He came back
to the ground.

And he whispered...

And you flew up in the air
With that big silly bird.

Is that how it happened?
Or is that just absurd?

Tell me, do you remember?
Do you remember this day?

Will you remember the fun?
And the play?

What was your favorite
part of today?

I remember... it was...

Well, it's getting late now.
This day was fun.

Dinner is over.

We said,
"Goodnight, everyone."

This is our special time.

It's the end of the day.

We've cleaned up the room.

Put the toys all away.

And we rock in our chair.
No more games left to play.